BLAST TO THE PAST

#2

Disney's Dream

By Stacia Deutsch
and Rhody Cohon
Illustrated by David Wenzel

Aladdin Paperbacks
New York London Toronto Sydney

To all of our wonderful kids—we love you.

❧

ALADDIN PAPERBACKS
An imprint of Simon & Schuster Children's Publishing Division
1230 Avenue of the Americas, New York, NY 10020
Text copyright © 2005 by Stacia Deutsch and Rhody Cohon
Illustrations copyright © 2005 by David Wenzel
All rights reserved, including the right of reproduction
in whole or in part in any form.
ALADDIN PAPERBACKS and colophon are registered trademarks of
Simon & Schuster, Inc.
Designed by Lisa Vega
The text of this book was set in Minion.
Manufactured in the United States of America
First Aladdin Paperbacks edition June 2005
2 4 6 8 10 9 7 5 3
The Library of Congress Control Number 2004109146
ISBN 0-689-87025-6

Contents

1

Monday Morning

The car screeched to a stop in front of West Hudson Elementary School.

"Hurry up, Abigail," my sister commanded. "You're going to be late to meet your teacher."

I checked the dashboard clock. I had plenty of time. CeCe just wanted to get rid of me.

I leaned over to tie my shoe. Not because it needed to be tied, but just to bug her.

I peeked in my backpack to make sure that the time-travel computer was hidden safely inside. I looked inside my homework folder. Then, I took out my coin purse and counted my money. I put the coin purse back and finally zipped up my backpack. After all that, I slowly opened the car door and stepped out onto the sidewalk.

The instant I closed the door, CeCe sped off, leaving a cloud of dust behind her.

I was brushing off my pants when my friend Bo came up beside me.

Bo's real name is Roberto. He's the new kid at school.

"Hey, Abigail!" Bo pointed at the car. We heard the tires squeal as CeCe left the parking lot. "What's your sister's rush?"

"CeCe got her driver's license this year," I answered. "Mom lets her drive the car because she works at a movie theater after school." I slung my backpack over one shoulder.

"Oh, yeah. I see her there all the time. The Happy Times Movie Theater," Bo said, tipping his own backpack onto its wheels. "I like that place. On Mondays, they charge nineteen-twenties prices."

"Yeah. Well, Mom said since CeCe has the car today, she had to drop me off early this morning. There is nothing CeCe hates more than driving me places."

"Does she always zoom off like that?" Bo asked. He was talking pretty loudly—for Bo. He used to be so shy and quiet that I could barely hear him. But ever since we'd time-traveled together, he'd gotten a little louder. Or else I'd developed supersonic hearing.

"Yep. She wants to get away from me as fast as she can." I thought about all the other times she'd rushed me out of the car. "We don't get along. In fact, she tattles on me all the time. She's always trying to get me in trouble." Sometimes I think Bo is really lucky to be an only child.

"What do you do about it?" Bo asked.

"I work extra hard to make her crazy. I tell on her too. We're in a big war." I smiled mischievously. "I can be really annoying when I want to be."

"You definitely annoyed her today," Bo said, and laughed a little laugh. Then he said, "Don't you think it's weird that Mr. C wants us to meet him in the gym before school? I mean, I'm never up this early."

Mr. Caruthers is our third-grade social studies teacher. He's so cool, we call him "Mr. C."

"Yeah," I agreed. "It's weird. I thought I was in trouble when he called me at home yesterday. Then I found out he called the twins, too."

We headed around the back of the school building.

"Mr. C told my mom we were going to have a special History Club meeting this morning," Bo said with a wink.

We knew what "History Club" meant. It's what we like to call our time-traveling adventures.

Of course, we'd only had one History Club meeting so far.

I patted the outside of my backpack, thinking about the time-travel computer inside.

Last Monday, Mr. C had given us the computer. When we put a special cartridge into its back, a glowing green hole opened up in the floor. We jumped in. And that's how we traveled through time. Taking the cartridge out brought us home again.

When he first handed us the computer and cartridge, Mr. C explained that, for some reason, famous Americans from the past were giving up their dreams. They weren't inventing, speaking out, or fighting for what was right. They were quitting!

A sticker on each cartridge showed us who we were going to visit. Our mission was to make sure that the person didn't quit! The tricky part was that we only had two hours to get the job done.

Our first mission had been a total success. We visited Abraham Lincoln in 1862 and convinced him to issue the Emancipation Proclamation, which he did—on September 22, 1862.

I pulled my backpack closer and made a wish: "I hope this History Club meeting means we get to time-travel again today," I whispered so softly, no one could hear me.

Then, in my normal voice, I asked Bo, "Where do you think the twins are?" Jacob and Zack were in our class and lived next door to me.

Bo shrugged. "Maybe they're already inside," he said.

Someone had propped the gym door open. We let ourselves in.

Jacob and Zack were waiting for us by the basketball hoop. When I saw them, I started to giggle. Soon, I was laughing so hard that my eyes filled with tears.

Jacob and Zack were wearing red-and-purple-striped sweatpants with matching hooded jackets. I see Jacob and Zack every day at school and on weekends, too. The twins hadn't dressed alike since kindergarten. They looked ridiculous.

Jacob gave me a mean look. "Stop it!" he demanded. "Grandma sent us new clothes." He sighed a big sigh. It was the kind of sigh you make when you really have no choice.

"Mom said we had to wear them," Zack added, tugging at the zipper on his jacket. It was jammed. "I think I'm going be stuck wearing this forever," he moaned.

At that moment, Mr. Caruthers walked into the gym.

"Hey! Look at Mr. C!" I pointed at our teacher.

Mr. C was wearing a suit and a bow tie. His hair was neatly combed. His shirt was tucked into his

pants. Even his glasses were sitting nicely on his nose.

"What's the deal?" Zack asked in surprise. "He's usually a wreck on Mondays."

When Mr. C came to class on Monday mornings, his suit was *always* crumpled, his hair *always* stuck up, and his glasses were *always* crooked.

"Hmmm," Bo muttered, scratching his chin. He does that when he's thinking really hard. "Something weird is going on."

"I'm glad you all could make it," Mr. Caruthers said to us. "Follow me." We walked across the gym to the back stairs. "This way." Mr. C disappeared down the stairs. "Are you coming?" he called up to us.

I had never seen anyone go near the steps at the back of the gym. It was dark down there. If a basketball bounced down those steps, there was not one kid in the whole school brave enough to go get it.

By the look on Bo's face, I knew he wasn't going to be the first to go down the stairs. Not because the basement was creepy, but because Mr. Caruthers was down there. Bo might talk a little louder to us kids, but he was still really nervous around adults.

I was curious. But not curious enough to go down to the super-scary basement.

We all stood around, silently staring at the stairwell.

Finally, Jacob moved forward and said, "If I can jump into a green glowing hole and time-travel, I can walk down the gym stairs." Jacob is always ready for an adventure.

"If I can wear this stupid sweat suit in public," Zack said, "I can definitely go into the basement." He followed Jacob. I was surprised because Zack is never very brave.

Once there were other kids in the basement, Bo was willing to go. "Come on, Abigail. We have to go if we want to time-travel again," Bo said, as he disappeared into the darkness.

"Okay," I told myself, "the faster I go down, the sooner I can come back up."

My heart was racing as I jumped onto the first step.

2

Invention

I leaped down the stairs two at a time until I reached the bottom.

It was really dark. The pipes were clinking. There was a soft hissing noise. And my heart wouldn't slow down.

Mr. C was standing in front of a huge wooden door. Slowly, he took a key out of his pocket and put it into the lock. The sound of the doorknob turning echoed in the hallway. A rush of cool air made the back of my neck tingle.

There was a strange sucking noise behind me. I tightened my hand into a fist. Then I heard another weird, breathy sound. My fingernails dug into my palm.

And finally:

"Achoo."

I screamed!

Zack started to laugh. "Did you think I was a ghost?" he asked, sneezing again.

"I'm not afraid of ghosts," I lied.

"So why'd you scream?" Zack asked in a haunting voice.

"Just 'cause," I said, not wanting to admit how really scared I actually was.

When Mr. C went inside and turned on the light, I felt better. We all followed him into the room.

The first thing I noticed was a long worktable. Pieces of plastic and bits of wire were scattered all over the table. Tools were everywhere. There was a box sitting on the floor.

"Cool." Jacob looked at our teacher like he was a hero. "You're an inventor!" Jacob was sort of an inventor too. He loved computers and spent hours taking them apart, changing them, and putting them back together.

Mr. C smiled. "This is my workshop." He picked

up the box from the floor and set it on the table.

We gathered around the table to see what Mr. C was doing. "What kind of stuff do you invent?" I asked.

"Top-secret stuff," he answered with a wink. "Jacob, did you bring the computer I gave you?"

"I gave it to Abigail for safekeeping. Zack and I have a monster living at our house," Jacob explained.

"Gabe's not a monster," I told Mr. C. "He's just a toddler. But he does like to break stuff." I took the computer out of my backpack and handed it to our teacher.

"Smart kids," Mr. C said as he put the computer down on the table. "It could be dangerous if the wrong person finds the time-travel machine," he warned.

"Where'd the machine come from?" I asked.

"A long time ago," Mr. C began, "I decided that I wanted to invent a time-travel machine."

"Did you think you could do it?" Zack asked. He rolled his eyes and sighed. "Even though I've time-traveled, I still can't believe the thing really works!"

"I didn't know if I could do it, but I decided to

try," Mr. Caruthers said, while he pulled a wad of blue and white wires out of the box and began untangling them. "The first computer I made was kind of like the one I gave you, but bigger and heavier. I painted the outside of it bright red." He put all the white wires back in the box.

"What happened?" Jacob asked.

"Big Red worked the first time I tried it. But after two trips to the past, it broke. I couldn't figure out the problem, so I made another computer. Big Blue was a little faster and not as heavy. It was great until I dropped it coming home from seventeen seventy-six." Mr. C handed me the blue wires and showed me how to twist them into curlicues. "I lost Big Blue somewhere between seventeen seventy-six and today. I never saw it again."

I looked over at our computer sitting on the table and asked, "What do you call this one? Big Black?"

Mr. C chuckled. "No. I call it 'Molly,' after my mom." Suddenly, his eyes turned dark and he became serious. "There is one strange thing about this computer."

"What one thing?" I asked as I got to work twisting wires.

He sighed. "Ever since I invented this new model, everyone I meet is about to quit." He reached into his pocket and pulled out a small, thick notebook. "I never had that problem with Big Red or Big Blue." He handed me the notebook. "I made this list when I first invented the time-travel computer. It's a list of all the people in American history I wanted to visit."

I looked down the list of names. I recognized a lot of them from social studies class. Mr. C pointed at the name Thomas Edison. "Here's where things changed," he told us. "Before Thomas Edison, all of my time-travel visits were to people who were working hard, pursuing their dreams. When I visited Mr. Edison with the newest computer, however, he told me he was quitting."

Jacob looked up at the brightly glowing lightbulb. "I guess you convinced him not to quit, right?"

"Yes," Mr. C responded. "But from then on, everyone on the list has had to be convinced to keep working. Every week I have to visit someone else. So far, with a lot of hard work and a little bit of luck, I've been able to keep history on track."

"What happens if you don't visit them? Or if you can't convince them?" Zack asked. He sounded a little nervous about the answer.

"Have you ever heard of James Smooter and the Smacktell?" Mr. C asked.

We all shook our heads.

"Once, I took a week vacation and James Smooter and his invention disappeared from history." There was a sorry look on Mr. C's face.

"What's a Smacktell?" Jacob asked.

Mr. C shook his head. "I don't want to talk about it," he said sadly.

I flipped through the notebook. Mr. C wasn't even halfway through his list. "Isn't it weird that all the people on your very own list are quitting?" I asked.

"Yes," Mr. C admitted.

I started to ask another question when Bo timidly asked, "Why would anyone want to quit their dreams?"

"Sometimes, things get rough," Mr. C answered.

"It's hard. You feel like your idea won't work. Or that people will laugh at you. Or someone tells you that you should quit." He took the blue wires from me.

"I don't get it," Zack said. "Why would anyone give up working on something they really want to do? No matter what happened"—he wrinkled his forehead—"I'd never quit trying."

"What are you talking about?" Jacob poked his brother in the arm. "You quit everything. Remember soccer? Piano lessons? Cooking classes?"

"Boring, boring, and super boring." Zack yawned. "Dad says I'm still experimenting. I just haven't found the right activity yet. He says when I find the one I'm supposed to do, I'll stick with it."

"I bet you'll never find one that you like," Jacob said.

"I will too!" Zack shoved his brother.

"Will not!" Jacob grabbed Zack around the waist.

"Boys! Stop fighting!" Mr. Caruthers said. They acted like they didn't hear him. Zack knocked Jacob to the floor, and they rolled like a log to the center of the room.

Mr. C looked at me. I shrugged. "Sometimes they're best friends," I explained. "Sometimes they're not."

"I know just what to do," Mr. C said with a twinkle in his eye.

The boys kept wrestling.

Mr. C quickly wrapped the blue wires around a computer chip, then put the wires and chip into an open cartridge. "Hang on tight," he said as he put the cartridge cap on and snapped it into place.

The last thing I remember was Zack shouting, "Will too!" Then, the explosion hit.

The boom was so huge, things fell off the table. Screws and nails rolled onto the floor. It was like a huge earthquake and tornado had slammed the room at the same time.

And when it was over, Jacob and Zack weren't fighting anymore. They were sitting on the floor, jaws hanging open, frozen like statues.

My hair was sticking up all over the place. Bo's T-shirt was untucked and hanging out of his jeans.

Mr. Caruthers stood behind his workbench. His suit was a mess. His hair was sticking up to the sky.

And his glasses had slipped way down on his nose. Now he looked like it was Monday.

"I don't understand why it has to explode like that, but I just can't figure out how to make a time-travel cartridge without the blast," Mr. C said, holding the cartridge up to the lightbulb for a better look. "Someday I'll figure it out."

"Excellent!" Zack suddenly cheered, interrupting Mr. C's thoughts.

We turned our heads to see what had happened to Zack. He was holding his hooded sweatshirt high above his head. The explosion had freed his zipper. And the fight with his brother was totally forgotten.

"Do you kids want to time-travel again?" Mr. Caruthers asked us.

"Yes!" Jacob, Zack, and I shouted together. "Yes," Bo said softly at the same time.

Mr. C looked at a clock on the wall. "There isn't enough time left this morning. We'll have to continue our History Club meeting later." He tucked the computer and cartridge into his suit pocket. "Let's meet in my classroom after school."

As we all walked back up the gym stairs, I realized I still had a few questions left.

"Why are *you* quitting?" I asked our teacher.

Mr. C tilted his head and looked at me out of one eye. "I'm not quitting, Abigail," he said. "You kids are helping me while I work on a different, very important project. That's why I wanted to show you the lab and how I make the cartridges."

I really wanted to know more, but we were already at the top of the gym stairs.

"Go to class," Mr. C told us. "I'll meet you there."

Then, our teacher turned and disappeared back down into the basement.

3

Time Travel

It was the longest school day of my life. When it was finally over, Jacob, Bo, Zack, and I met outside Mr. Caruthers's classroom. Jacob had taken off the purple-and-red-striped hooded sweatshirt from his grandmother, but Zack was still wearing his.

"Is it stuck again?" I asked, pointing at the silly looking jacket.

"Nah," he answered. "But I'm starting to like it."

I scrunched up my face. It was hard not to laugh when I looked at that jacket. Even harder when I looked at the matching pants. I slapped one hand over my mouth while Jacob knocked on Mr. C's classroom door.

We waited. There was no answer. Mr. C wasn't there.

I looked up and down the hall, but there was no sign of our teacher.

"I think we should wait out here." Zack put his hands on his hips and puffed out his chest.

I tested Mr. C's doorknob. It wasn't locked, so I opened the door a crack. "I say we go in. Maybe he left the computer and cartridge for us."

"We already know where we're going," Jacob agreed. "We're going to meet Walt Disney."

Every Monday, Mr. Caruthers asked our class a new "what if someone quit?" question. All the kids in my class love to imagine what the world would be like without electricity, airplanes, or any of the ideas that have changed America.

Now that we had time-traveled, Bo, Zack, Jacob, and I knew that the questions Mr. C asked in class weren't made up—someone was really going to quit, and change history forever. So, in social studies this morning, when Mr. C leaned back on his desk and asked, "What if Walt Disney had quit and never made *Steamboat Willie*?" we knew we were going to visit Walt Disney after school.

At first I thought the question was silly. Who'd ever heard of *Steamboat Willie*? I knew Walt Disney. He created Mickey Mouse, Minnie Mouse, Pluto, and Disneyland. But who cared about *Steamboat Willie*?

By the end of class, I knew I was wrong. Everyone cared about *Steamboat Willie*.

Steamboat Willie wasn't a person. It was the name of a cartoon.

Mr. C told us that before Walt Disney made *Steamboat Willie*, all cartoons were silent. Characters would move their lips like they were talking, but no words came out. Almost all movies were silent too. Sometimes there would be words on the screen to read. Or a piano player playing mood music. But mostly, the movie theater was a quiet place to go.

Walt Disney took *Steamboat Willie* and added music and voices. The voices and music were recorded directly on the film and synchronized, which means the sound matched the action perfectly. It was something new and very exciting. And after Walt Disney added sound to *Steamboat Willie,* everyone wanted sound with cartoons.

So what would the world be like without *Steamboat Willie?*

Ryota Yoshida thought there would be no Mickey Mouse.

Mr. C told the class that he agreed with Ryota. He explained that Walt Disney first showed *Steamboat Willie* on November 18, 1928. That day is known as Mickey Mouse's birthday. Without *Steamboat Willie,* Mickey Mouse probably wouldn't be so popular.

Max Cohen said he thought that without *Steamboat Willie* there'd be no Disneyland Resort, Walt Disney World Resort, Walt Disney movies, or the Disney Channel on TV.

Bo leaned over and whispered to me, "The Walt Disney Company is so big, they even own stuff we don't think about."

"Like what?" I whispered back.

"Like other television stations, restaurants, and

cruise ships." Bo likes to read and he knows a lot about everything.

"Wow!" I said, still whispering so our teacher wouldn't hear. "Walt Disney started so many things! If he had quit and never made *Steamboat Willie*, the world would be a lot less fun." I raised my hand to tell Mr. C what Bo and I had talked about.

But he called on Jackie Thompson next. Jackie said that if Walt Disney hadn't made *Steamboat Willie*, all cartoons might still be silent.

I dropped my hand because I knew in my heart that Jackie was right. If Walt Disney had quit, not only would the world be less fun, but it would be worse than that! If he'd quit, there would be a Global Cartoon Disaster! I couldn't even imagine it. No *Steamboat Willie* meant that on Saturday mornings we'd be watching cartoons without sound.

We had to convince Walt Disney not to quit. And fast!

"We're wasting time!" I said, pushing the classroom door wide open. "Mr. C might never come. Let's get the computer and cartridge. We need to get started."

"No," Zack argued. "Without Mr. C, we don't know where we are going." He stepped forward to block the doorway into Mr. C's classroom. Zack was serious about waiting.

I ducked around him and went inside anyway. The boys all followed, even Zack.

I opened Mr. C's desk drawer and found the computer and cartridge inside. "Look!" I cheered. "Here it is!" I took out the computer and handed it to Jacob.

I held up the cartridge. It had a small sticker of Mickey Mouse on it. "And here's the proof we need to convince Walt Disney not to quit!"

"I don't think this is a good idea," Zack pleaded with Jacob. "We can't just take the computer. It isn't ours. Plus, if Mr. C wanted us to have it, he wouldn't have asked Abigail to give it back to him this morning."

But Jacob wasn't listening to his brother. He turned the computer on and asked me for the cartridge. Jacob wasn't going to miss a chance to use the computer again. Mr. C had given Jacob a wristwatch to keep track of our time on our last mission. Jacob got the watch out of his pocket and put it on.

Jacob and I were ready to go.

I turned to look at Bo. So far, he hadn't said a word. I wanted to know what he thought we should do. "Should we go, or should we wait for Mr. Caruthers?" I asked him.

Bo rubbed his chin. "I think we should go," he said at last. "If we waste any more time, we might miss our chance."

Zack was outnumbered three to one.

Bo, Jacob, and I put our backpacks in a corner. I took out my coin purse and stuck it in my pocket. Just in case.

Jacob slipped the cartridge into the back of the computer. A big, green hole opened next to Mr. C's desk. Smoke spilled out over the floor.

Jacob jumped eagerly into the hole. Bo followed him.

Zack stepped back. I wasn't sure if he was going to come or not.

"Let's go, Zack," I said. "You have to come. We're a team." I snagged his backpack out of his hands and put it next to mine.

"What if Mr. C gets here and figures out that we left without talking to him?" he asked.

"When we get back, we'll tell him that we convinced Walt Disney not to quit. Mr. C will be proud." The green hole was getting smaller. If we waited any longer, it would close.

Zack took one final look toward the door. "I guess you're right. He's not coming." He sighed. "But I'm not going with you." He went to get his backpack.

"Oh yes, you are." I shoved him hard. He stumbled forward and fell into the hole.

Then, I leaped in after him.

4

New York City

"You are blocking the screen!" a voice shouted.

"Get out of the way!" another voice called out.

We were standing on the stage of a huge movie theater. I'd never seen such a big theater in all my life. There must have been close to two thousand seats. All full of people. Angry people who wanted us to get off the stage.

"We cannot see the movie!" a lady shouted. I turned to look at the screen. Sure enough, there were four big shadows covering the bottom half of a very tall movie screen. I waved my arms a little bit and made a shadow bunny with my fingers. The crowd didn't like it. They were booing and yelling at me.

Before I could say anything, Jacob grabbed my arm

and pulled me to the side of the stage. There was a roar of applause from the audience. And then, their applause died down, and people began to laugh.

I poked my head around the side of the screen so I could peek at the movie. There was a man in a black coat and hat walking a tightrope. Monkeys were crawling all over his back. The crowd was going crazy with laughter and clapping their hands like they'd never seen anything so funny in their lives.

Mr. C had told us that movie theaters in 1928 were mostly quiet places because the movies had no sound. But that wasn't true. Sure, the movie didn't have any talking or singing, but there was a live band in front of the stage playing music. The audience was laughing really hard. And cheering.

The theater was full of noise.

I had to admit the movie was funny. I would have stayed there watching if Bo hadn't poked me in the arm.

"This isn't a Mickey Mouse movie," Bo said, deep in thought. "This is a Charlie Chaplin movie. I've seen this one a million times."

"I told you we shouldn't have come," Zack complained. "And I wouldn't be here at all if Abigail hadn't pushed me into the hole." He gave me a very mean look.

When Zack wasn't mad, he was very funny. I thought about the movie and realized that Zack reminded me a little of Charlie Chaplin. They both could make me laugh out loud. Too bad he was in such a horrible mood. I hoped he'd snap out of it soon.

"We should have waited for Mr. C to tell us what to do," the not-funny, very cranky Zack whined.

"Look at this!" Jacob called. He pointed to a poster near where we stood. It read:

**Now showing at the Colony Theater:
Charlie Chaplin in The Circus.
September 18, 1928. Tickets: 15 cents.**

Bo came and stared at the poster. "Hmm," he mumbled, rubbing his chin. "Something isn't right."

"It's the price!" I exclaimed. "You can't even buy a candy bar for fifteen cents. It must be a mistake."

"No . . . ," Bo said, continuing to stare at the poster. "In nineteen twenty-eight, it cost fifteen cents to see a movie. That's not the problem."

"See?" Zack grumbled. "Even Bo knows that something is wrong. We should go back to school and wait for Mr. C."

"We're already here," Jacob told his brother. "We've got to find Walt Disney and get him to show *Steamboat Willie* today so that Mickey can have his birthday."

Zack just grunted.

With one last, long look at the poster, Bo said, "We're wasting too much time standing around. Let's go."

We walked around the backstage area looking for Walt Disney. I'd seen a picture of him in class but wasn't sure if I would recognize him.

In the picture, Walt Disney was thin and tall. His dark hair was cut short and smoothed back. He had on a dark business suit with a long tie. And he had a skinny little mustache.

When we were onstage, I'd seen a lot of people in

the audience. I checked out the people working backstage at the movie theater. But so far, no one looked like Walt Disney.

After a few minutes of searching, I gave up. "We have to go ask for help," I told the boys. "Who's going to do it?"

I looked at Bo. He shook his head.

I looked at Zack. He was still grumbling and muttering about how we shouldn't have come.

Jacob had stopped to check the computer. He was concentrating on the screen.

That left me.

A man was rushing by, a long cord in his hand. He was wearing a tag that said, HARRY REICHENBACH, PROMOTER.

I hurried after him. I had to jog to keep up.

"Excuse me, Mr. Reichenbach." I had to take two steps for every one of his. "Why isn't *Steamboat Willie* showing today?"

He didn't answer. He just kept on walking.

"Excuse me," I said again. "Is Mr. Disney here today? We have to find him. It's very important."

He stopped. And stared at me. When his mouth finally opened, he spoke so fast, it was hard to tell where one word stopped and another started. "Whatso important?" he asked.

"Walt Disney has to show *Steamboat Willie* today. History will forever be changed if he doesn't," I explained.

The corners of his mouth rose at the edges, and his eyebrows scrunched up. It was something between a smile and a frown. "Whatso special about *Steamboat Willie*?" he asked.

"It's the first successful animated cartoon with sound recorded on the film." The words were spilling out of my mouth in a single breath. "It's about this mouse named Mickey. It's going to change the way the world sees animation. And"—I inhaled—"it will make Walt Disney famous." All that took about a second to say. I was talking just like Mr. Reichenbach.

There was a glimmer in Mr. Reichenbach's eyes. "Well," he said, "Mr. Disney is not famous yet, because I have never heard of him. Or of a cartoon called *Steamboat Willie*. And I've heard of everyone and everything in this business." Before he turned to leave, he asked, "Are you sure the movie is supposed to be shown at the Colony Theater today? There are a lot of other movie theaters in town."

I looked at Bo. He was the only one who'd know the name of the theater where *Steamboat Willie* was shown. He nodded.

"Yes," I said. "The movie was—I mean is—supposed to be shown today at the Colony Theater."

"Sorry, kids," Mr. Reichenbach apologized and hurried off, disappearing down a long hallway.

"I knew it!" Zack stomped his foot. "Even the promoter of the Colony Theater hasn't heard of Walt Disney! What's a promoter, anyway?"

"He's the guy who does advertising," Bo explained.

"Maybe he can help Walt Disney promote *Steamboat Willie*," I suggested. "That is, if we ever find Walt Disney."

Jacob was still holding the computer, looking at the numbers on the screen. "September eighteenth, nineteen twenty-eight," he said to himself. Then, he pressed a button. "New York City." He shook his head. "I don't get it! We're right where we're supposed to be."

Bo just stood there, rubbing his chin and mumbling, "Something isn't right."

Bo was in his own world. I didn't want to interrupt him, so I turned to Jacob instead. "How much time do we have left?" I asked. We had to pay attention to our two-hour time limit. None of us knew what would happen when the time was up. And we didn't really want to find out.

Jacob checked Mr. C's wristwatch. "We've wasted fifteen minutes."

"We need a plan," I suggested. "I think we're going to have to go out on the streets of New York to find Walt Disney."

"Abigail's right!" Suddenly, Bo grabbed my hand and dragged me back to the movie poster behind the screen. Jacob and Zack had to run to keep up. Bo pointed at the poster. "We have to go find Walt Disney."

"I don't get it," I said, leaning in to look at the poster more closely.

Bo stuck his finger on the date.

"September eighteenth, nineteen twenty-eight?" I asked.

Jacob got the problem before I did. "Didn't Mr. C say that *Steamboat Willie* was first shown on *November* eighteenth, nineteen twenty-eight?"

"Yes," Bo confirmed. "November eighteenth is Mickey Mouse's birthday."

"No wonder no one has heard of Walt Disney or seen *Steamboat Willie*." I bit the inside of my lip. "We're at the Colony Theater two months too early!"

5

Walt Disney

"Oh, man." Zack leaned forward and banged his head against the movie poster. "Ouch!" he muttered. Then he slammed his head against the wall.

"Stop it!" I shouted at him. "What are you doing? You're going to hurt yourself."

"I am trying to knock some sense into my head," he replied. "What am I doing here? I should still be at school waiting for Mr. C."

"Relax," Jacob commanded, grabbing his brother's shoulders to stop him from hitting his head a third time. "We still have an hour and twenty-three minutes. Plenty of time to find Walt Disney and convince him."

"Convince him to do what?" Zack grumbled as he

turned to face his brother. "We don't know what he needs to do. We don't even know if he's in New York City at all!"

Zack had a good point.

"Hang on!" Bo said suddenly. He was rubbing his chin so hard, I thought it might break off. "I have a biography about Walt Disney at home." He paused and became very still. We stood silently, waiting for Bo to finish thinking. "I remember reading that *Steamboat Willie* was shown on November eighteenth, nineteen twenty-eight, but that the sound was recorded—" Suddenly Bo's eyebrows lifted and he opened his eyes really wide. "The sound was recorded on September eighteenth, nineteen twenty-eight!"

"Holy cow!" I exclaimed. "That's today. We don't need to convince Walt Disney to *show* his movie. We need to convince him to *record* the sound for it!"

"Didn't Mr. C ask us in class, 'What if Walt Disney quit and never *made* the movie?'" Zack threw up his hands in frustration. "We would have known what we needed to do if we had just waited for him to explain."

"It might have saved us some time," Jacob admitted. "But now that we know what we have to do, let's go find Walt Disney. He must be at a recording studio around here somewhere."

Just then, I noticed Mr. Reichenbach was heading back our way. I had an idea. But I had to act quickly. The man was zooming past us faster than a speeding bullet.

"Excuse me," I said, stepping boldly in front of him. He had to stop or else he would have run me over.

"Youstillhere?" he asked, his feet grinding to a stop. "Still looking for a man and a mouse movie?"

I smiled. "Yep, but we're in the wrong place."

"Where do you wannabe?" Mr. Reichenbach asked.

"We think Walt Disney is at a recording studio somewhere. He is recording the sound and voices to his movie today," I said.

"Well then, there are two recording studios nearby. Close enough to walk to." He gave us directions and sped off down the hall.

"Way to go, Abigail," Jacob congratulated me. "Let's make tracks!"

We rushed out the door and down the street.

The first studio was closed. "Let's go to the next one," I said. We didn't want to waste any more time, so we started running.

Zack was dragging a little ways behind us, whistling, "Heigh ho. Heigh ho. It's off to find Walt Disney we go." Now he was double annoying: He was complaining *and* he was singing songs from Disney movies. I turned my head and called over my shoulder, "Hey, Dopey. Hurry up!"

"I'm not Dopey," he replied, taking a few big steps to catch up. "I'm still Grumpy." I had to admit that, even when he was driving me crazy, Zack could still make me laugh.

We ran for two blocks and then turned a corner. SMACK. I crashed into a short, round man. I slammed into him so hard, his hat fell off. "Sorry," I apologized, picking up his hat and brushing it off. "Did I hurt you?"

"No." The man laughed. He had bushy hair and

a great big mustache. In his hand was a violin case. "No harm done," he said, taking his hat and putting it back on. "Are you all right?"

I told him I was fine. "Is that a violin?" I asked. And before he could answer that question, I asked another: "Are you in a band?" And another: "Who do you work for?"

He tucked his violin case under his arm. "You certainly are inquisitive, aren't you? Yes, this is a violin. And I am in an orchestra." He answered my first two questions.

He walked to the door of the second recording studio Mr. Reichenbach had told us about. Just before he went inside, he turned and said, "Oh, I nearly forgot. I work for Mr. Walt Disney." The door closed behind him.

"Ha! Ha!" Jacob cheered. "We found Walt Disney. He's here!" He grabbed me around the waist, lifted me up, and spun me around. "Abigail, you're too cool!"

Bo put his hand on my shoulder. "You have the magic touch," he said. "I wish I could talk to adults like you do." It felt good to get such nice compliments from my friends.

There was a teenie weenie smile at the corner of Zack's mouth. "We had to find him eventually," he said with a wink. "You know, it's a small world after all."

I shook my head and laughed.

We went inside the recording studio. The light in the room was dim but not dark.

There he was! Walt Disney looked exactly the same as in the pictures we'd seen of him in class. He was standing behind a microphone.

Beside him was a band. Seventeen musicians and a conductor. I saw the violin player I'd run into. He was sitting in the front row. I waved, and he waved back.

There were more men roaming around the room. Some were lugging wires. Others were moving big boxes. A woman in a yellow coat and matching hat was writing on a notepad. A man in a white shirt was sitting next to a large black box.

I nudged Bo and pointed at the box. "The recording machine," Bo whispered. "That guy's the sound man."

I nodded.

"And look there," Jacob said excitedly. "That's *Steamboat Willie!*"

I looked where Jacob was pointing. A movie was playing on a screen against the back wall. I immediately recognized Mickey Mouse. He was banging and playing on a cow's teeth like xylophone keys.

The movie was exactly the same as when we'd seen it in Mr. Caruthers's class!

We watched for a little while. The movie was super funny. But very quiet.

Walt Disney stood in front of a microphone and announced that the musicians were ready to record the sound.

"Everything seems to be going just fine," I said to Jacob. "Everyone is working. No one is quitting. So why do you think we're here?"

Zack sighed and said, "Next time, we could ask Mr. C."

"Stop moping, Zack. It's too late to ask him. We're already here," Jacob said. Then he told us to stand back against the wall so we'd be out of the way. "In class, Mr. C told us that *Steamboat Willie* is only seven minutes long. Let's hang out and see what happens."

Walt Disney pointed at the screen and gave the conductor some last instructions. Then, the film started over at the beginning.

It felt like something magical was about to happen.

Walt Disney had put little balls of light on the film. Each time a little light appeared, the conductor matched up the music to the film. The first few minutes of the recording were perfect.

But in the middle of the film, the balls of light started coming faster and faster. They were too fast. The conductor couldn't keep up. The musicians lost the pace. The music didn't match the action.

All of a sudden there was a loud, low *blat* from a tall, stringed instrument. "Stop! Stop!" the sound guy yelled. "We blew out a tube in the recording machine."

"Another?" Walt Disney gasped. "That's the third one today. How many do we have left?"

"We have only one more," the sound man told Mr. Disney.

Walt Disney looked at the conductor and said very seriously, "Make certain that we get it right this time. A little softer on the bass fiddle, please."

They started the movie from the beginning again. It was right on. I swear, the music was coming right out of the cow's tail. Walt Disney performed the sound of Mickey Mouse. His squeak was perfect. It was awesome. I could see how this movie changed animation history.

They were near the end of the recording when Walt Disney tucked his hands up under his arms like a bird. A parrot came on-screen and opened its beak.

Walt Disney opened his mouth at the same time.

"Squawk," went Walt Disney. "Squawk," went the parrot.

"Stop the recording!" the sound man shouted over the orchestra. The movie stopped playing. The orchestra stopped. Walt Disney stopped. We froze too.

The man turned to Walt Disney. "Nice squawk, but you blew out the last recording tube."

Walt Disney ran a hand through his hair. He lowered his eyes and shook his head. Then he sighed loudly.

"I quit."

6

The Future

I didn't even think. "You can't quit!" I shouted.

It took Walt Disney a second to figure out where I was standing. "What do you mean?" he asked with a very serious look on his face. "I just quit. And that is final!" He looked around the room at the musicians. "What are you waiting for?" he demanded. "Start packing! I have no more money to pay you, so you might as well go home."

The musicians started gathering their equipment.

"No!" I blurted. "Mickey Mouse is going to be huge." The conductor gave me a puzzled look. "Trust me," I said. "Mickey Mouse will be everywhere! People will have Mickey Mouse T-shirts, watches, and dolls."

"My grandma gave me Mickey Mouse underwear last year," Zack tacked on to my list.

"Tell them about the animation," Bo reminded me in a soft voice.

"Yeah," Jacob added. "This isn't all about Mickey Mouse."

How could I have forgotten the most important part? It was up to me to make sure the Global Cartoon Disaster didn't happen!

"All cartoons after *Steamboat Willie* will have sound recorded on the film," I told Walt Disney. My voice echoed through the now silent studio. "There will be animated movies in the theater and on TV. Some TV channels will show only cartoons all day long. Twenty-four hours a day of just animation." I would have gone on, but everyone in the room was looking at me as if I'd just grown a second head.

Bo leaned in. "Abigail, you're talking about the future. They just don't get it. These people don't even know what a TV is."

Walt Disney didn't bother walking over to where we were standing. He just spoke in a loud, clear voice from the other side of the recording studio. "Do you children know how hard it is to record sound on film?" he asked. "I came all the way to New York because there are no recording studios that can do this in Los Angeles. I have spent every last dime trying to make this work."

He squinted his eyes at us. "I don't know who you children are or how you got in here, but you saw the recording. It was a disaster. I will never show this film until it is perfect. Never! The way it is now, the sound doesn't always match the action. Plus, we've just blown out my last and final recording tube. I cannot afford another one. It is over."

Bo whispered in my ear. I repeated to Walt Disney what he said: "I know you sent a telegram to your brother, Roy, asking him to sell your car. When that money comes, you'll try again—right?"

"How do you know about my car?!" Walt Disney wanted to know.

I quickly turned to Bo. "How do I know about the car?"

"I have that biography about Walt Disney at

home, remember?" He pulled up his shoulders and hunched down his neck. "I read about it."

I couldn't tell Walt Disney that Bo had read about him in a book. It wouldn't make any sense. I wasn't sure what to do next.

Zack suggested we tell Walt Disney that we came from the future. Jacob agreed, but he wanted to wait until there weren't other people around.

"Can we go outside?" Jacob asked Walt Disney. "Let's go where we can talk in private."

Walt Disney said no.

Jacob told him it was important.

He still said no.

"Now we do it my way." Zack pushed in front of Jacob. "After I convince him, we can go back to school." He rose up on his tiptoes to be a little taller.

In front of all the musicians, the conductor, and the technical crew, Zack told Walt Disney all about the time-travel computer. He told him that we'd come to convince him to finish *Steamboat Willie*. And, of course, he told him how we hadn't waited for our teacher to tell us what to do.

I couldn't tell if Walt Disney believed Zack or not, but he was listening.

"You should have waited," Walt Disney agreed. "You are wasting your time trying to convince me. I am not going to try again. I am finished."

Zack nodded. "I know how you feel. Once I quit something, I never want to try it again either."

It was weird. We were in a room full of people, but it seemed like Zack and Walt Disney were the only two in the room. It was like they were best friends or something.

"I used to have a successful cartoon character," Walt Disney told Zack. "His name was Oswald the Lucky Rabbit. One day my partner, Charles Mintz, told me I didn't own Oswald. He took the cartoon and most of my staff. He's still making silent Oswald films. And getting paid!" Walt Disney waved his arms around the room. "Now I am stuck with a mouse movie. And I cannot record the sound because I have no more money."

"What about putting the sound on a record?" Zack suggested.

"Yes. A lot of people are trying that," Walt Disney replied. "But the records get bumped or scratched. Or they melt because they are made of wax. The sound hardly ever synchronizes correctly." He made a clicking noise with his tongue. "I want the sound and the cartoon to fit perfectly together. For me, using a record would be worse than not having any sound at all. The sound has to be on the film, or I'm not doing sound."

Zack thought about it and asked, "Can you keep *Steamboat Willie* a silent film? Would anyone buy it?"

I gasped. It wasn't our job to help him quit! I tapped Zack on the shoulder. He ignored me.

"I have two other Mickey Mouse cartoons I've been working on back in Los Angeles with my friend Ub Iwerks," Walt Disney answered. "I guess I could finish them, then see if I could sell all three together as silent short films." He turned away and started gathering his equipment.

Jacob grabbed Zack and hauled him into a private corner. Bo and I followed.

"Zack, what are you thinking?!" Jacob asked in a tight, shaky voice.

"If the man wants to quit recording sound, let him," Zack answered calmly. "So *Steamboat Willie* won't be the first sound-on-film animation. Maybe someone else will make cartoons with sound." Zack looked at Jacob and said, "Without *Steamboat Willie*, the world won't fall apart."

"No, but it won't be very much fun," Jacob challenged. "*Steamboat Willie* was just the beginning of everything Walt Disney did!"

"Give it up, Jacob. He quit. What do you want to do? Take Walt Disney to the future?" Zack asked with a half-laugh. "Maybe we can take him to Walt Disney World and show him a good time in Fantasyland." Zack snickered at his own joke.

"Hmm," Bo mumbled. He was rubbing his chin. "Not a bad idea, Zack. Last week we took Abraham Lincoln to the future, and that worked out really great. Let's try taking Walt Disney to the future too."

"I was just kidding," Zack insisted, but Bo wasn't listening.

"How about Disneyland?" Bo muttered to himself. "It was his first amusement park." He scratched his chin a little harder. "Or maybe Walt Disney Studios. That's where his movies are made." Bo asked Jacob how much time we had left.

"Forty-eight minutes," Jacob told him.

"Where can we take him in such a short amount of time?" Bo sucked in a deep, thoughtful breath and exclaimed, "I've got it!" He didn't mean to talk so loudly, but Bo was so excited, his voice echoed throughout the studio. He blushed.

"What?" all three of us asked at once.

"What?" Walt Disney asked from the other side of the room.

"What?" all the musicians asked together.

"Do you guys have something you can do for a minute?" Bo asked everyone. "I need to talk to my friends." Bo's face was a little red. I think he surprised himself when he spoke so loudly.

While Walt Disney and his musicians continued packing up to leave, Bo pulled us deeper into the corner and whispered, "We have to get Walt Disney outside alone so we can take him to the future. He has to see how *Steamboat Willie* will change the world."

"Where are we going?" I asked.

"The Happy Times Movie Theater," Bo said. "There's a movie he needs to see."

"Can't we go somewhere else?" I asked. I was nervous about going to the theater where CeCe works. Taking Walt Disney there was risky. If CeCe thought something was suspicious, she'd tell on me and try to get me grounded. That's how the war between us worked. "I don't want to risk running into my sister," I told the boys.

"Sorry," Bo said. "The movie he needs to see is at the Happy Times Movie Theater this week."

"Maybe we can rent the DVD," I suggested. "The Happy Times Movie Theater only shows old movies." Scratching my head, I added, "I've never understood why people want to go to a theater to see a movie they could rent at the store."

"Seeing a movie on DVD isn't the same as seeing it on the big screen. I think the big screen is way better," Bo explained. "If we can show Walt Disney just a few minutes of the movie, I think it'll be easy to convince him to finish recording sound for *Steamboat Willie*."

"Let's hope it'll be a quick trip," I said, agreeing to go.

"If we're lucky, CeCe won't even know we're there," Jacob said as he took the computer out of his pocket and programmed it to take us directly to the movie theater.

"Wait a second." Zack jumped into the conversation. "I was just kidding. I didn't really want to take Walt Disney to the future."

"But it was a good idea," Bo responded.

"I don't want—," Zack began to protest.

"We're going to need your help to do it," Bo interrupted. "Walt Disney likes you. You're the only one who can convince him to come outside with us."

"I'm not—," Zack started again.

I cut him off. "Please, Zack. It's up to you," I pleaded. "We're in this together. Making a cartoon with sound is Walt Disney's first big dream. After he finishes *Steamboat Willie,* he'll dream bigger and bigger."

When Zack didn't say anything, Jacob added, "Mr. C sent us to save history. Don't you want to tell him we succeeded? We can't do this without you."

Zack sighed a big, long sigh and finally gave in. "Okay, you win. I'll help out the team. Mr. C is counting on us, so let's give it our best shot." He went across the room to get Walt Disney.

We went outside. Bo stood guard at the studio door. I looked up and down the street to make sure no one saw us.

After a few minutes, Bo said, "Get ready. Here they come."

The instant Zack and Walt Disney stepped out the studio door, Jacob pulled the cartridge out of the computer. The green glowing hole opened in the pavement.

As soon as the hole was big enough, Zack and Jacob each grabbed one of Walt Disney's arms and tumbled into the hole together.

Knowing we were going to the Happy Times

Movie Theater was making my stomach hurt. "I just hope we don't run into CeCe," I said as Bo took my hand in his.

Bo counted to three, and we jumped.

On four, we landed, because time travel is really fast.

7

Snow White

We landed in the lobby of the Happy Times Movie Theater.

Walt Disney looked really confused. And he had a lot of questions. I like it when a person has a lot of questions.

"Where are we? How did we get here? What is this place?" He didn't give us a chance to reply. "It looks like a movie theater, but what are these posters?" He was standing by a long wall covered with movie posters. "I've heard of Buster Keaton and Greta Garbo, but never John Wayne or Frank Sinatra."

He dragged his finger across the last poster in the hall. "And who made *Snow White and the Seven Dwarfs* into an animated movie?!" The last question wasn't really a question but a demand.

I was about to answer but didn't get the chance.

"You did," Bo said. "We brought you to Happy Times to see the movie on this poster."

I stuck my finger in my ear to clear out the wax. I had to make sure I heard him right. Bo never talks loudly. And never, ever to an adult. "What are you doing?" I asked him.

Bo looked at me and said, "Since it was my idea to come here, I should be the one to show Walt Disney his future."

I patted Bo on the back. "Go for it!"

"You made *Snow White and the Seven Dwarfs*," Bo told Walt Disney while pointing at the poster on the wall. "It was the first feature-length animated film. *Snow White* was released four days before Christmas in nineteen thirty-seven. We brought you here to see the movie."

"I did?! If I made the story of *Snow White* into a movie, I think I'd remember." Walt Disney snorted. "Oh, I nearly forgot. You're showing me the future." He still thought we were making up a wild story.

Walt Disney studied the theater lobby. The theater was built to look like an old-time movie house, so he didn't see anything too modern. The carpet was red velvet. There was a chandelier hanging from the lobby ceiling. All the decorations were old-fashioned. Not necessarily from 1928, but close enough.

Walt Disney looked around again and said, "If we are in the future, then the world has not changed at all."

Zack suggested that we take Mr. Disney to the bathroom and show him the automatic flushing toilets. Bo reminded Zack that this trip was about movies, not potties.

"I do not understand how we left the recording studio," Walt Disney said. "But I have no money, no job, and nothing to do. If you children want to pay for me to relax and see a movie, I will not argue. As much as I like entertaining other people, I love to be entertained myself."

"Good thing I brought my coin purse," I said as I headed to the ticket booth, leaving the boys to keep Walt Disney busy.

CeCe was at the ticket counter.

"Shoot!" I muttered under my breath.

"Hi," I said as cheerfully as possible. "I need five tickets."

"Aren't you supposed to be at History Club this afternoon?"

"It's a field trip," I said a little too quickly, shoving my money toward her.

Bo was right: On Mondays, the theater charged 1920s prices. Each ticket cost only fifteen cents.

CeCe put the money into the cash register and pulled the tickets out of the machine. "You'd better be telling the truth," she said as she separated our tickets. "I'm going to tell Mom and Dad I saw you here. And if you're lying, you're going to be busted for skipping club time. You'll be grounded for life."

"You do that and I'll tell Mom what really happened to her knitting." I grinned. "We'll be grounded together." I didn't give her a chance to respond. I rushed off to give my friends their tickets.

When we entered the theater, the movie had already started. The mean queen was speaking to

her magic mirror. When she asked the mirror who was the fairest one of all, Walt Disney cried, "I cannot believe it!"

"What's he so upset about?" Jacob asked me. I had no clue.

"Charles Mintz beat me to it!" Walt Disney shouted at the screen. A family in the front row turned around to see what was going on.

"What is he talking about?" Jacob asked Bo softly.

"Charles Mintz was the guy who took his Oswald the Lucky Rabbit cartoon," Bo reminded us. "Other than that, I don't know." He looked at Walt Disney, who was now standing up and shouting at the top of his lungs.

"He synchronized the sound! He even made the movie in color!" Walt Disney had moved into the aisle. "Where is the record player?"

A woman asked Walt Disney to please be quiet. He wouldn't. Then, she said she'd call the manager if he didn't sit down. He ignored her and started moving toward the screen.

I was about to follow Walt Disney down the aisle

when Bo said, "This was my idea. I have to be the one to explain to him why we brought him here." I hung back and let Bo go talk to Walt Disney.

"There's no record. The sound is on the film," Bo told him. "And it's not Charles Mintz's film. It's a Walt Disney movie. We're in the future, remember?"

"I do not believe you," Walt Disney exclaimed, turning around. "I want to see the record player!" Then, without another word, he rushed up the aisle, past Bo, and out of the theater.

We hurried out of the theater and into the hallway.

But it was too late.

Walt Disney was gone.

8

CeCe

I went left. Jacob sped right. Bo shot off toward the bathrooms. I had no idea where Zack went.

Now, along with my nervous stomachache, I had a splitting headache from worrying so much. What if CeCe ran into Walt Disney before we found him? If she talked to him, I was toast. CeCe loves movies and movie history. She would figure out who he was in a second.

I could never tell my sister about the time-travel adventures. There was no way I could explain it to her. Some kids talk to their brothers or sisters. They share secrets and stuff. I'd never told CeCe anything. And I didn't want to start with the most secret thing ever.

We had to find Walt Disney before she figured out what was going on.

Bo and Jacob came to tell me they hadn't found him yet. I was so stressed out, I thought I was going to explode.

Suddenly, Zack appeared at the top of the main staircase. He signaled for us to come up. "Walt Disney's up here. We gotta get him out of here before CeCe finds us."

Jacob and Zack knew how worried I was. They knew that I got grounded a lot because of her tattling.

As we went up the stairs, Bo asked me, "Why are you in a fight with CeCe?"

Jacob knew the answer. He started telling the story. "A few months ago, Zack and I were playing at Abigail's house. We saw CeCe take the car without permission."

I finished explaining. "I told my parents, and CeCe got grounded. She couldn't drive for a whole month. It's been war ever since. I tell on her. Then, she tells on me. So, I tell on her again." We got to the top of the stairs. "If she finds out about Walt Disney, I'm doomed."

Bo looked over his shoulder. Now he was nervous about seeing my sister too.

Zack met us in front of a small doorway. There was a sign with bright red letters on the door that said, PROJECTION ROOM NUMBER 3.

Zack pushed the door open just enough to let us in. It swung closed behind us.

I hoped Walt Disney had seen enough of the future to be convinced to finish *Steamboat Willie*. CeCe might be wandering around the building. We had to get out of there quickly. I was wondering if I was strong enough to tackle Walt Disney and shove him back through the green hole, when Jacob asked, "What are you doing?"

"I was planning—," I began, but Jacob cut me off.

"Not you." He pointed at Walt Disney, who was on his knees between a large film projector and a big silver disc where a long strip of film was winding in slow circles. "Him. What is Walt Disney doing?"

"I am looking for the record player, of course," Walt Disney answered. "I cannot understand how Charles Mintz got the sound to synchronize with the film." He crawled on his knees to a nearby cabinet and checked inside. "The record player must be here somewhere."

Bo likes to read, but Jacob knows stuff about electronics. Not just computers, but all electrical things.

"There's no record," Jacob insisted. "You have to believe us."

"*Snow White and the Seven Dwarfs* is your movie," Bo added, in case Walt Disney had forgotten.

"Come on, you guys. Let's cruise," I said anxiously. I expected CeCe to walk in at any second.

"I need one more minute," Jacob told me. "I think I can convince Walt Disney if I show him how this projector works."

"I'll go peek out the door," Zack suggested. "Then, I can warn you if I see her."

"Okay," I told Zack, then turned to his brother. "But Jacob, you have only one minute." I held up one finger to make it clear.

"No problem," Jacob said.

Zack moved over by the door while Jacob pressed a bright red button on the movie projector. The film stopped. The sound stopped too. Walt Disney was amazed. "No record?" he asked Jacob. "Really?"

"Really," Jacob said, grinning. "The sound is on the film. Turn off the film—"

"Turn off the sound," Walt Disney finished Jacob's sentence. "How was the movie sound recorded?"

"Moviemakers use a machine kind of like your recording machine," Jacob began. "Only instead of recording tubes, we use microphones and something called a computer."

"No tubes?" Walt Disney asked.

"No tubes," Zack confirmed quickly, poking his head back into the room. "Got it?" Zack peered out the door again. "Jacob, the coast is clear. If you're done explaining the projector, we should go back to nineteen twenty-eight."

A voice suddenly shouted from the movie theater below: "Turn the movie on!"

"Yeah," another voice called out. "We paid good money to see this film."

"Someone should get the manager," I heard a woman say.

"Want to try?" Jacob stepped back so Walt Disney could run the projector. He showed him the buttons that ran the projector. Jacob let Walt Disney press a shiny green button.

There was a little window looking into the theater below. Bo peeked out. "The film is back on," he reported.

"Aha! The sound is working again too. Now I understand how this works!" Walt Disney pressed the red button. The movie stopped again. The sound stopped too. He pressed the green button. The movie started. The sound started. Red. The movie and sound stopped. Green. The movie and sound started.

After he'd played with the buttons five or six times, Walt Disney exclaimed, "What do you know?! The sound really is on the film."

"I told you so," Jacob said with a grin. Just then, an angry roar came from the theater below. Everyone was shouting for someone to turn the movie on and leave it alone.

"I will fix it," Walt Disney said. He hit the green button one last time. And from the theater, we heard a booming cheer and happy applause when the movie started going again.

All of a sudden Zack slammed the projection room door closed and ran into the center of the room. "She's headed this way," he announced, waving his arms wildly. I didn't have to ask who "she" was. "What do we do?" Zack asked.

"I can't possibly explain all this to my sister. We have to get out of here!" I panicked. "Jacob, get the computer."

Jacob tried to help. He whipped the computer from his pocket, but the cartridge dropped out onto the floor.

Walt Disney picked it up. "Look," he commented. "There's a very small picture of my Mickey Mouse on this thing."

"Yeah," I said. "There's a picture of Mickey. Now, give Jacob the cartridge," I begged. "Please, we don't have any time."

I heard CeCe's voice in the hallway. "What's going

on in there? No one is supposed to be up here."

Bo pointed to the door. It was inching open.

"Please," I begged Walt Disney. "Don't let her find us here. Give Jacob the cartridge. Let's go."

Walt Disney just laughed. "The future is wonderful. Where I come from, there are no computers. There is no color. I cannot even get synchronized sound for *Steamboat Willie!*" He slapped his hands together. "Why should I go back at all? I have so many dreams I've never even talked about. In this time, I could do it all. In nineteen twenty-eight I was just a small-time cartoonist who drew a little mouse named Mickey," he said. "And no one cares about Mickey Mouse!"

"Everyone cares about Mickey Mouse," CeCe said as she stormed into the room. She caught my eye and glared at me. My life was over. I knew I was in big trouble.

"How do you know about Mickey Mouse?" Walt Disney asked, pointing at CeCe.

CeCe didn't answer. She looked at me. "I expect some answers, Abigail. You'd better tell me what this has to do with a History Club field trip." She waved her hand around the projection room. "You kids are not supposed to be in here. And you"—she pointed at Walt Disney—"you shouldn't be touching the projector."

"I—," I began. "I mean we—" I was stumbling over my words. I didn't know what to say. CeCe and I never talked, and I wasn't sure how to begin.

Walt Disney saved me. "How do you know about Mickey Mouse?" he asked my sister again.

"I'm not done with you." She narrowed her eyes at me. "Or you. Or you. Or you." She poked her finger at each of the boys. We were all really scared. Now I wasn't going to be the only one busted. She was going to take my friends down too.

CeCe turned to face Walt Disney. She took off her old-fashioned movie-theater jacket. Underneath she was wearing a T-shirt with a picture of Mickey Mouse on the front.

"Everyone knows about Mickey Mouse." She looked at each of us as she spoke. "Since this is a History Club meeting, you probably already know that 'Mickey Mouse' was the code word for the most historic American invasion during World War Two."

"The invasion at Normandy," Bo supplied. Reciting facts calms him down.

"World War Two?" Walt Disney looked surprised. "Wasn't one world war enough?"

"That's another story," Bo interrupted. "Just know that in our world, Mickey Mouse is way more than a cartoon mouse."

Walt Disney was silent for a second, then said, "I've been to the future. I've heard sound on film. I've watched *Snow White*. And I've even seen a Mickey Mouse shirt. You children have convinced me. Now, I want to finish my movie. But before we go, I have one last question." He turned to CeCe, who was still standing by the door. "Are you certain Charles Mintz wasn't the first to put sound with animation?" Walt Disney asked her.

"Who's Charles Mintz?" CeCe asked.

Walt Disney smiled. "That does it. I have to go and add sound to *Steamboat Willie*." He headed out the projection room door. "Take me home."

"We'd love to," I said, thinking this was the way I'd

escape my sister. I stepped forward, but something was holding me back.

It was CeCe. She was holding on to my sleeve and wouldn't let go. I twisted and turned, but she wouldn't open her fist.

"Where do you think you're going?" she asked me in a low voice. "The boys can go. This is between you and me."

The boys wanted to stay with me. "Let's drop him through the hole," Zack suggested, tilting his head toward Walt Disney. "He can get back himself. We should stay with Abigail."

"No. Go on ahead," I told Zack. "I'll meet you behind the theater in two minutes. If I'm not there, leave without me." They didn't want to, but I convinced them to go outside. They left.

Even after we were alone, CeCe wouldn't let go of my sleeve. "That man is Walt Disney, isn't he?"

I sighed. It was no use lying. I was in trouble, anyway, I might as well tell the truth. But I didn't have to spill everything. I'd simply answer her questions and then try to get outside as fast as I could. "Yes," I said.

"You must have brought him here from the nine-teen twenties. But I don't know how you did it."

"It was nineteen twenty-eight," I smugly corrected her.

"I bet this has something to do with Mr. Caruthers, doesn't it?"

I nodded.

CeCe sighed and wrapped my sleeve more tightly in her fist. "When I was in his third-grade class, we all knew he was an inventor. But we didn't think he'd ever made anything that worked."

"Maybe that's what he wanted you to think," I said rudely.

CeCe looked confused, so I explained all about Mr. C and the time-travel computer. "But there is a glitch in the cartridge," I told her. "We only have two hours to convince Walt Disney to make *Steamboat Willie*. We've almost used up all our time. In twelve minutes, we have to be back at school."

"The movie is seven minutes long," CeCe reminded me. "That means he has to get it right this time!"

Suddenly, my sister let go of my sleeve. And just as

I was wondering if I should make a break for the exit, she said four words I never thought I'd hear: "Let's call a truce."

"What?" I asked. "You want to end the war? You aren't going to try to get me grounded anymore? Are you feeling okay?"

CeCe took her hand and smoothed the fabric of my T-shirt. "You know how important old movies are to me. The day Walt Disney recorded the sound on *Steamboat Willie* is one of the most important events in animation history." She looked me straight in the eye. "I want to come with you."

I raised one eyebrow and looked at her sideways. I couldn't believe my ears.

"I'll never be mean to you again. And I won't tell anyone about this History Club field trip. Not ever. You have to believe me." CeCe gave me a big smile and added, "I'm your sister, after all."

I was too stunned to speak. I stared at my sister. Then, she said, "I'm sorry for all the times I got you in trouble."

I knew that just because she said she was sorry

didn't mean that she and I were suddenly friends. But it was enough for now.

"Yeah," I replied. "I'm sorry too." I motioned toward the door. "Come on. Walt Disney is waiting."

9

Sound

"What's she doing here?" Jacob asked the second CeCe and I walked into the back alley. He was pointing at my sister.

"CeCe, go visit with Walt Disney," I told her. "I'll explain it to the boys."

My sister went over to talk to Walt Disney, who was standing by some trash cans. She'd covered up her T-shirt with her theater jacket. She looked like she belonged with Mr. Disney in 1928.

Once we were alone, I explained, "She's coming with us."

"Are you sure?" Bo asked. I nodded.

"I thought you didn't like her." Zack looked at Jacob.

"I thought you two didn't get along." Jacob looked back at his brother.

"We called a truce." I shrugged. "The war is over."

"She's been pretty mean to you lately," Jacob reminded me.

I looked over at my sister and gave her a thumbs-up. Turning back to Jacob, I said, "Yeah, but I was mean to her too. We're okay now."

"Well, then," Jacob said, looking around to make sure the coast was clear, "let's get out of here." He slipped the cartridge into the back of the computer. The time-travel hole opened in the sidewalk. Walt Disney didn't hesitate. He was the first to jump into the green glowing mist. Jacob, Zack, and Bo followed.

"Are you sure you want to come?" I asked my sister.

Without answering, she took my hand. And together, we jumped.

We landed on the sidewalk in front of Walt Disney's recording studio. Musicians were filing out onto the street, musical instruments in their hands.

"Where do you think you are going?" Walt Disney asked them.

"You sent us home," the violinist replied.

"No one is going home," Walt Disney said, pulling the studio door open and holding it. "Everyone, go back inside."

"John and Ralph already left," a man with a trumpet case said.

"Paul left too," another man added. "They said you cannot pay us—"

"*Hakuna matata,*" Zack interrupted, flashing a smile. "It means 'no worries.' Walt Disney will have the money by the end of the day."

Walt Disney laughed and mussed Zack's hair "*Hakuna matata,*" he repeated with a wink. Then Walt Disney headed inside to find out how to get a new recording tube.

Bo turned to Jacob. "How much time do we have left?"

"Twelve minutes," Jacob answered.

We hurried inside.

Walt Disney was standing alone in the back of the room. He had a piece of paper in his hand. When we got close, he handed it to Bo. It was a telegram that said Roy Disney had wired Walt Disney some money. "You were right. Roy sold my car," Walt Disney said, sighing sadly. "I loved that car."

"Soon, you will be able to buy another one," Bo said. "Lots and lots of new cars."

Walt Disney took back the telegram. "That's the future. This is now. Selling my car gave me just enough money for one more shot. The sound man found another recording tube in a box in the closet. One more chance is all I get."

"Then get it right," Zack said. "You can do it! You'd better do it! It's bad enough that we have to tell our teacher we left without talking to him. We'd better be able to tell him you finished *Steamboat Willie.*"

Walt Disney started thinking. He was rubbing his chin, just like Bo. "I know how to fix the problems with the music. I will explain to the conductor how to better synchronize the sound. But how do we keep the recording tube from exploding?" he asked softly, under his breath.

"Can you use this?" Zack asked, tugging at his red-and-purple-striped sweatshirt. "Maybe if you muffle

the really loud sounds during the recording, it won't explode."

"That is a fine idea," Walt Disney agreed. "I can place the shirt in the bass fiddle to soften the boom, and I can squawk with less gusto. It just might work." Walt Disney pointed at the sweatshirt. "May I borrow your jacket?"

Zack tried to take off the sweatshirt, but the zipper was stuck—again.

"*Hakuna matata.*" Walt Disney gave Zack a pat on the back. "I'll borrow something from the sound man." And he rushed off.

"Looks like I might have to live in this sweatshirt forever." Zack tugged at the zipper.

"Yeah," I said. "But if your idea saves the recording, I might buy myself a sweatshirt to match."

"Eight minutes," Jacob announced.

The lights dimmed.

The film started.

From where we stood I could see a white shirt stuffed into the bass fiddle. And the sound man's bare chest.

The film started, and the conductor signaled the orchestra to begin playing. This time, everything went smoothly. The characters really looked like they were moving in tune to the song. When Mickey Mouse opened his mouth, Walt Disney made him squeak. When Mickey Mouse cranked the cow's tail, it was like the music was coming from the cow. And when the parrot squawked, nothing exploded.

"Cut!" the sound man yelled just after the film ended. The room fell silent. We were waiting to hear how the recording went. The musicians stared at the sound man. Walt Disney stared at the sound man. All of us kids stared at the sound man too.

"Perfect," the man said at last. "Not even one mistake! We did it!"

Everyone cheered!

"I'm so glad I got to be here," CeCe told me. "I'll never forget this day."

We headed toward Walt Disney to congratulate him, but a strange beeping noise from the computer stopped us.

"What's that sound?" CeCe asked.

Jacob looked at the computer. "It's a timer."

"There wasn't a warning alarm last time we used this thing," Zack said.

"Mr. C must have added it," I guessed. "Maybe that's why he asked me to give him the computer back this morning."

"Thirty seconds," Jacob announced reading the numbers. "Twenty-nine. Twenty-eight. Twenty-seven."

We waved good-bye to Walt Disney from across the room and hurried toward the back door.

"Whereya going?" a man asked as we rushed past. It was Harry Reichenbach. He was leaning against the wall.

"We're late for school," I answered. It was pretty much true. We had to get back to school—in our own time.

"Well, hurry on," Mr. Reichenbach said, opening the door for us. "And hey, thanks for telling me about *Steamboat Willie*. I already scheduled it to open at the Colony Theater on November eighteenth. I just have to convince Walt Disney."

"Five hundred dollars should do the trick," CeCe said. "For a two-week showing."

"That's a lot of money," Mr. Reichenbach said. "A whole lot of dough."

"It's fair," CeCe said. "This movie will make history."

"I think you may be right," Mr. Reichenbach said with a laugh.

Outside the studio, Jacob pulled the cartridge out of the computer. The time-travel hole opened in the sidewalk, spilling green glowing smoke all over the street.

"We have fifteen seconds!" Jacob announced. He jumped into the hole with Bo and Zack close behind.

"Hey, CeCe," I said as we stepped up to the edge of the green hole, "why did you tell Mr. Reichenbach to give Walt Disney five hundred dollars? Wouldn't that have been a ton of money for people in nineteen twenty-eight?"

"I know a little about the old movies," CeCe said with a grin. "Five hundred dollars was a lot of money back then, but that's how much the Colony Theater paid for the first two weeks of *Steamboat Willie.*"

"It was worth it!" I said. "I'm glad you came along," I told her.

The green hole was shrinking fast.

"Thanks, Abigail," she said. And I could tell she really meant it.

I took my big sister's hand in mine and, together, we jumped home.

10

Mr. Caruthers

We landed in the girls' bathroom.

"There has to be a way to tell the computer where we want to be when we get back to school," Zack complained. "It's going to ruin my reputation if someone sees me coming out of the girls' bathroom." He checked to make sure there wasn't anyone hiding in the toilet stalls.

"What reputation?" Jacob laughed so hard, he snorted.

It didn't matter, anyway, because there was no one else around. We were the only ones in that part of the school.

Out in the hall, the boys headed toward Mr. C's

classroom. I stayed behind a second to say good-bye to my sister. "Bye," I said.

"Yeah." CeCe opened her arms as if she was going to give me a hug. But she didn't. "I'd better get back to work," she said, stuffing her hands deep in her pockets instead. "It's a long walk."

"Okay." I stuck my hands in my pockets too. "See ya."

"Yeah," CeCe said. She turned and walked away.

I watched her go and wondered what would happen when we saw each other at home later. "*Hakuna matata*," I said to myself. "At least we have a truce." I headed off to Mr. C's classroom.

The boys were waiting for me outside. The door was closed.

Jacob knocked on the door.

We waited. There was no answer.

I looked up and down the hall, but there was no sign of our teacher—again.

"I think we should wait out here." Zack put his hands on his hips and puffed out his chest.

I tested Mr. C's doorknob. It twisted easily. "I say we

go in," I countered. "We should put the computer back."

It was already a little after five o'clock. The twins' mom would be waiting with their little brother in the parking lot. It was time for us to go.

"No," Zack argued. "Mom and baby Gabe can hang out for a few. We have to wait for Mr. C. He should know that we saved history!" He stepped forward to block the door into Mr. C's classroom. "Maybe we should run down to his laboratory."

"You don't have to go to the laboratory," a voice echoed in the hallway. "I'm not there."

"Mr. Caruthers!" I gasped. "We were just talking about you. Where have you been?"

"I was busy," Mr. C said mysteriously. "I told you I had important things I was working on." We moved out of the way to let Mr. C into his classroom. Then, we followed him. "You should have waited for me after school. I was only five minutes late."

"See?" Zack began. "I told you—"

Mr. C interrupted him. "Should we see how you did?" He pulled a book off the shelf and handed it to me. I read the title out loud: "*The People Who Shaped America*." We use this book in class all the time.

"Turn to page fifty-six," he told me. There was a picture of an old movie poster from *Steamboat Willie*. It was cute. Mickey Mouse was wearing a little black hat and was steering a boat. He was smiling, and I could hear his voice in my head. And if I closed my eyes, I could imagine Walt Disney recording Mickey's squeaks.

"It's a great poster," I said. "But there's no date on it." I was suddenly really nervous. What if something had happened after we left? What if the recording got lost? Or erased? Or wasn't perfect, like we'd thought? What if the movie wasn't ready to open on November eighteenth?

"Good thinking, Abigail," Mr. C told me. He reached into his desk and pulled out a white envelope. "I found something to help you know if you succeeded or not. If you really saved history, there are two newspaper articles inside." He handed me the envelope.

"And if we failed?" Zack asked.

"I guess there'd be nothing inside," Bo said. "Abigail, open the envelope."

I stood there staring at the envelope in my hand. I wondered if there was anything inside.

"You're taking too long." Jacob snagged the envelope out of my hand. "Just open it already."

I tried to grab it back. Jacob wouldn't let go.

"Be careful," Mr. C warned.

"Let go," I told Jacob. "You're going to rip it!" But it was too late. The envelope tore in half.

A small piece of paper fluttered to the ground.

Zack was the fastest. He picked up the piece of paper. It was a bit of newspaper, old and yellowed at the edges.

"'*New York Times.* November eighteenth, nineteen twenty-eight,'" Zack read out loud. "'*Steamboat Willie* is an ingenious piece of work with a good deal of fun. It growls, whines, squeaks and makes various other sounds.'"

"Hey, look," Jacob said suddenly. Stuck inside the half of envelope he was holding was a second magazine clipping. It was from the *Exhibitor's Herald.* He handed it to Bo.

Bo read: "'It is impossible to describe the riot of mirth, but it knocked me out of my seat.'"

"What's 'mirth'?" I asked Mr. Caruthers.

"Ask Bo," Mr. C told me. "He knows."

"It means it made him laugh," Bo explained. "A lot."

"Well, then," I said, "these prove that we did it! We convinced Walt Disney to finish recording the sound. We kept history right on track."

I was just about to give Bo a big ol' high five when Mr. C said, "I'm glad it worked out, but you should have waited for me. I would have told you everything you needed for your mission."

"But—" I was going to say that we'd succeeded anyway, but Mr. C gave me a stern look, so I stopped talking.

"Because you didn't wait, you must write a five-page essay," he said. "I want you to write about your dreams. And how you are going to work on making them come true."

The four of us groaned loudly.

"Now that you've visited Walt Disney, do you know what a dream is?" Mr. C asked us.

"A dream is a wish your heart makes." Zack hummed a bit of the song from Disney's *Cinderella*.

Even when we were getting in trouble, Zack could make me laugh.

When Bo started to give the dictionary definition of "dream," I whispered to Zack, "How do you know that song? You've always said *Cinderella* is a girlie movie."

"Remember when we were little? You wanted to be Cinderella? I saw the movie at your house a bunch of times."

I was embarrassed. I remembered that I had worn a tiara every day for a month. I'd even slept in it. I'd definitely grown out of my dream to become a princess. Now I had bigger hopes and wishes.

"A dream can also be a goal or purpose," Bo said, finishing his definition.

"Good," Mr. C said. "Now that you all know what a dream is, you can write your essays."

"Oh, man," Zack complained to our teacher. "I shouldn't have to do this. I was the one who wanted to stay and wait for you. I told them a million times—"

"I understand, Zack," Mr. C said. "But I'm not going to change my mind."

Zack sighed.

Mr. C said, "You can give the essays to me next Monday at our History Club meeting. Let's meet in the library after school."

Jacob gave Mr. C back the computer and cartridge. Mr. C told him to hang on to the wristwatch because we'd need it again. We all got our backpacks. Then, Jacob and Zack went outside to meet their mom. Bo rushed off to get his bike. And even though the twins had offered me a ride, I decided to walk home.

I couldn't stop smiling. It had been an amazing day: We got up early. Saw Mr. C's workshop. Convinced Walt Disney to record sound on *Steamboat Willie*. And found out that we'd get to time-travel again next Monday.

When I got to my house, I stood outside and looked up at my sister's room. Her light was on. "I have a lot of dreams," I said to myself. "And maybe, someday, I'll share them with my sister CeCe."

But not tonight. Tonight, I was going to start writing an essay for my favorite teacher.

The B. S. Moss Colony Theatre was built in 1924 and was used as a movie theater for many years. This is a real picture of the theater just like it was when *Steamboat Willie* was first shown there. Almost two thousand people came on November 18, 1928, to see Walt Disney's movie and celebrate Mickey Mouse's birthday at the Colony Theatre. It must have been very exciting! Today, you can still visit the Colony Theatre in New York City. It is called the Broadway Theatre at 1681 Broadway and is now used for plays.

A Letter to Our Readers

Hi! We hope you enjoyed *Blast to the Past: Disney's Dream.*

Disney's Dream is not a true story, but it's not all made up either. The story is called "historical fiction," which means it's somewhere in between.

The time-travel part is fiction. We made that up because it is fun and exciting. But the part about how Walt Disney put sound on *Steamboat Willie*— well, that's true. And it is also true that *Steamboat Willie* changed the world of animation forever.

When Walt Disney first drew a picture of Mickey Mouse, he had big dreams for his little mouse.

In September 1928, Walt Disney went to New York City to record sound on the film of his new movie. The problems he had with recording the sound are all true. The recording tubes did blow out many times. Walt Disney even blew one out himself when he squawked like a parrot for the film. And Walt Disney did run out of money.

But it didn't really happen all in one day. It took

some time for Walt Disney to try recording again. And as far as we can tell, he never really considered quitting. Instead, he held on to his dream and let his brother, Roy, sell his beloved car in Los Angeles.

When Walt Disney got the money from the car sale, he tried again to record the sound for the movie. He kept trying until he got it right.

Steamboat Willie opened at the Colony Theater in New York City on November 18, 1928. Harry Reichenbach promoted the movie, and two weeks later the movie moved to an even bigger theater, called the Roxy. It was a huge hit!

There were other people making movies with sound at the same time as *Steamboat Willie*. *The Jazz Singer* was a talking film that came out in 1927 and ended the era of silent films. But when it came to cartoons, even though some of them had sound, the sound was on a record. No one had successfully put sound on the film of an animated cartoon before.

Steamboat Willie changed animation history, and Walt Disney started to dream even bigger. His dreams never stopped, and he never quit.

If you liked *Disney's Dream* and want to learn more about which parts of it are fact and which parts are fiction, or if you have a good idea for what the world would look like if Walt Disney had quit and never recorded sound on *Steamboat Willie,* visit our Web site at BlastToThePastBooks.com.

Enjoy!
—Stacia and Rhody

P.S. Watch for Abigail, Jacob, Zack, and Bo's next story, when they visit Alexander Graham Bell in *Bell's Breakthrough.*